The Lighthouse Keeper's Lunch

For Joss and Kate

Scholastic Children's Books,
Scholastic Publications Ltd,
7-9 Pratt Street, London NW1 0AE, UK

Scholastic Inc.,
555 Broadway, New York, NY 10012-3999, USA

Scholastic Canada Ltd,
123 Newkirk Road, Richmond Hill,
Ontario, Canada L4C 3G5

Ashton Scholastic Pty Ltd,
PO Box 579, Gosford, New South Wales,
Australia

Ashton Scholastic Ltd,
Private Bag 92801, Penrose, Auckland,
New Zealand

First published in hardback by André Deutsch Ltd, 1977
This edition published by Scholastic Publications Ltd, 1994

Text copyright © Ronda Armitage, 1977
Illustrations copyright © David Armitage, 1977

ISBN: 0 590 55175 2

Printed and bound in Spain
By Mateu Cromo, S.A. Pinto (Madrid)

All rights reserved

10 9 8 7 6 5 4 3 2

Ronda and David Armitage have asserted their moral right to be
identified as the author and illustrator of the work respectively, in
accordance with the Copyright, Designs and Patents Act 1988.

The Lighthouse Keeper's Lunch

Ronda and David Armitage

Hippo

Once there was a lighthouse keeper called Mr Grinling. At night time he lived in a small white cottage perched high on the cliffs. In the day time he rowed out to his lighthouse on the rocks to clean and polish the light.

Mr Grinling was a most industrious lighthouse keeper. Come rain...

. . . or shine he tended his light.

Sometimes at night, as Mr Grinling lay sleeping in his warm bed, the ships would toot to tell him that his light was shining brightly and clearly out to sea.

Each morning while Mr Grinling polished the light Mrs Grinling worked in the kitchen of the little white cottage on the cliffs concocting a delicious lunch for him.

Once she had prepared the lunch she packed it into a special basket and clipped it on to the wire that ran from the little white cottage to the lighthouse on the rocks.

But one Monday something terrible happened.
Mrs Grinling had prepared a particularly appetising lunch.
She had made . . .

A Mixed Seafood Salad

A Lighthouse Sandwich

Cold Chicken Garni

2 Sausages and Crisps

Peach Surprise

Iced Sea Biscuits

Drinks and Assorted Fruit

She put the lunch in the basket
as usual and sent it down the wire.

But the lunch did not arrive. It was spotted by three scavenging seagulls who set upon it and devoured it with great gusto.

"Clear off, you varmints," shouted Mr Grinling, but the seagulls took not the slightest notice.

That evening Mr and Mrs Grinling decided on a plan to baffle the
seagulls. "Tomorrow I shall tie the napkin to the basket," said
Mrs Grinling. "Of course, my dear," agreed Mr Grinling, "a
sound plan."

On Tuesday evening Mr and Mrs Grinling racked their brains
for another plan.
"They are a brazen lot, those seagulls," said Mrs Grinling.
"Brazen indeed," said Mr Grinling, "what shall we do?"
"Our cat does not appear to like seagulls," said Mrs Grinling.
"No, my dear," said Mr Grinling,
"Hamish is an accomplished seagull chaser."
"Of course," exclaimed Mrs Grinling,
"tomorrow Hamish can guard the lunch."
"A most ingenious plan," agreed Mr Grinling.

Hamish did not think that this plan was ingenious at all. He spat and hissed as Mrs Grinling secured him in the basket. "There, there, Hamish," said Mrs Grinling consolingly, "I'll have a tasty piece of herring waiting for you when you arrive home."

HAMISH

Sadly, flying did not agree with Hamish. His fur stood on end when the basket swayed, his whiskers drooped when he peered down at the wet, blue sea and he felt much too sick even to notice the seagulls, let alone scare them away from the lunch.

"Lackaday, lackaday,"
said Mr Grinling sadly.
"Miaow, miaow,"
agreed Hamish pitifully.

On Wednesday evening Mr and Mrs Grinling racked their brains again for a new plan. "What shall we do?" said Mr Grinling. Mrs Grinling looked thoughtful. "I have it!" she exclaimed, "just the mixture for hungry seagulls."

"Indeed, my dear," said Mr Grinling, "what have you in mind?" "Wait and see," said Mrs Grinling, "just wait and see."

"Mustard sandwiches," chuckled Mr Grinling
"A truly superb plan, my dear, truly superb."

On Thursday morning Mrs Grinling carefully packed the mustard sandwiches and sent them off down the wire to the expectant seagulls.

On Friday Mrs Grinling repeated the mustard mixture.

So, on Saturday, up in the little white cottage on the cliffs, a jubilant Mrs Grinling put away the mustard pot before she prepared a scrumptious lunch for Mr Grinling.

While he waited for his lunch down in the lighthouse on the rocks, Mr Grinling sang snatches of old sea shanties as he surveyed the coastline through his telescope . . .

"Ah well, such is life," mused Mr Grinling as he sat down to enjoy a leisurely lunch in the warm sunshine.